WHERE'S TIM'S TED?

First published in hardback in Great Britain by HarperCollins*Publishers* Ltd in 1999
First published in Picture Lions in 2000

3 5 7 9 10 8 6 4 2
ISBN: 0 00 664638 7

Picture Lions is an imprint of the Children's Division, part of HarperCollins*Publishers* Ltd.
Text copyright © Ian Whybrow 1999
Illustrations copyright © Russell Ayto 1999
The author and illustrator assert the moral right to be identified as the author and illustrator of the work.
A CIP catalogue record for this title is available from the British Library.
The HarperCollins website address is: www.fireandwater.com

Printed and bound in Singapore.

WHERE'S TIM'S TED?

Ian Whybrow

illustrated by Russell Ayto

Collins

An imprint of HarperCollinsPublishers

This is the farm where Tim's staying.

High in the sky is the moon.

Tim's got his jim-jams on.

It'll be bedtime soon.

Big kiss for Grandad.   One for Granny Red.

Tim says:

Excuse me,
where's my Ted?

Look behind the sofa.

Look behind the chairs.

"We'll find Ted in the morning. Time to go upstairs."

A funny thing happens in the middle of the night.
Tim says, "I think I'll see if Ted's all right."

This is the kitchen. No Ted in sight.

Pull

both

boots

on.

And into the moonlight.

Ben runs over.

Ben says, "Gruff!"

Tim says: Down, boy. Ssshhh, that's enough.

Tim shines his flashlight into the shed.

He whispers, "Excuse me, where's my Ted?"

The hens start clucking, "Ted, Ted, Ted?"

Tim says, "Ssshhh-ssshhh. Come and look instead."

They tiptoe to the stable. They whisper to the horse:

Pacer says:

Will you help us look for Ted?

Of course!

They creep to the cowshed. They whisper to the cows,
"Has anybody seen Ted?" But the cows only browse.

The ducks waddle down from the duck pond,

And the sheep flock along from the pen,

The goat butts in from the orchard,

All saying:

OY! WHAT'S GOING ON
HERE THEN?

Then very, very quietly... they creep towards the sty.

They find the piglets fast asleep,

With mummy pig nearby.

But wait, who can that be in mummy pig's bed?

Is it a little piggy? No...

IT'S TIM'S TED!

And the dog goes: Arf, arf, what a laugh!

And the chickens go: Cluck, cluck, what luck!

And the horse goes: Way-hay, I say!

And the cows go: Moo, boo, what a to-do!

And the ducks go: QUACK, QUACK, GIVE HIM BACK!

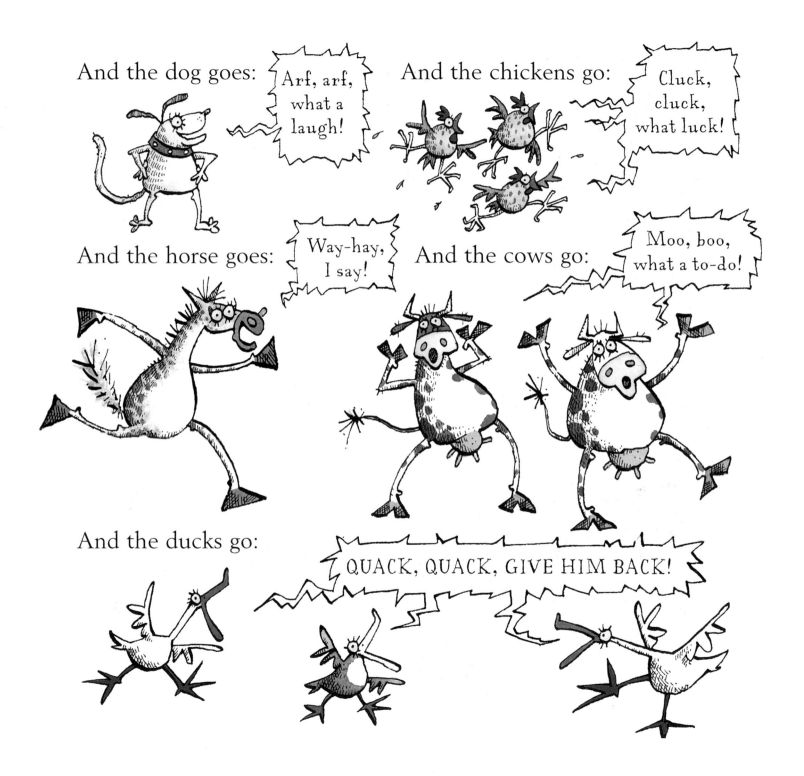

Tim says, "Calm down, calm down!
Be quiet for goodness sake!
With all that noise you're going to have
Granny and Grandad wide awake!"

"Now excuse me, Mrs Piggy,
But that's my Ted, I think."
Mrs Piggy says, "Oh, snort,
I thought he was mine, being pink."

Tim takes back his Ted.

Says thank you and crosses the yard.

He wants to turn the doorknob.

He tries, but it's too hard.

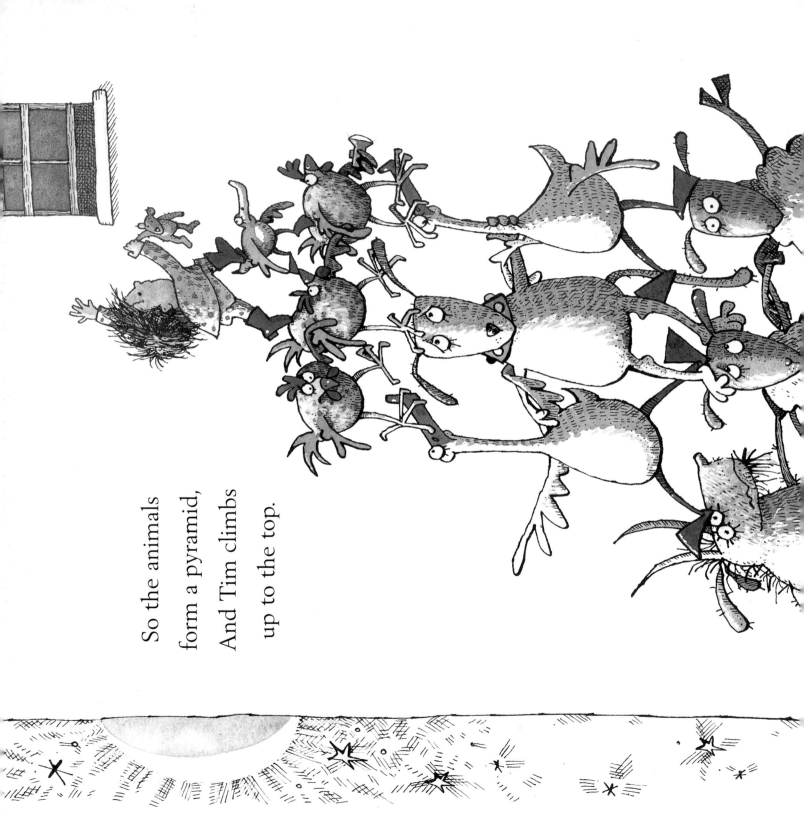

So the animals
form a pyramid,
And Tim climbs
up to the top.

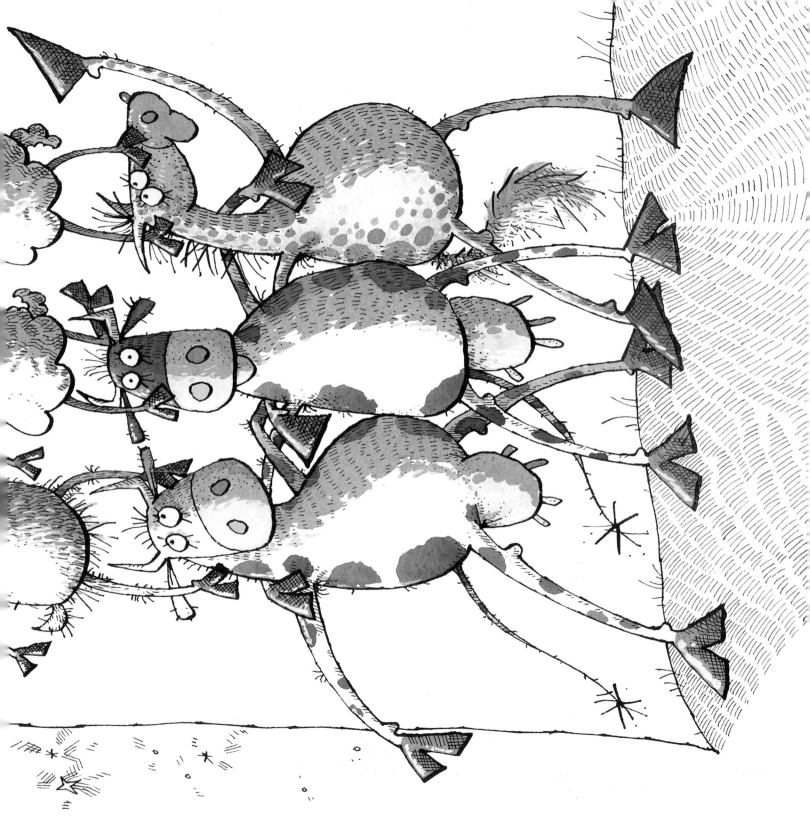

Jumps through his bedroom window.
Back into bed, 2-3-Hop!

Granny says, "Are you all right, Tim?"

But from Tim there isn't a peep.

He's tucked up tight with his old pink Ted.

And – guess what – fast asleep.